1. This book may be kept three weeks.
    It is to be returned on / before the last date
    stamped below.
2. A fine of 20p will be charged for every week
    or part of week a book is overdue.

Mr Tick the Teacher

by ALLAN AHLBERG

with pictures by
FAITH JAQUES

Puffin

Viking

PUFFIN/VIKING

Published by the Penguin Group
Penguin Books Ltd, 27 Wrights Lane, London W8 5TZ, England
Penguin Books USA Inc., 375 Hudson Street, New York, New York 10014, USA
Penguin Books Australia Ltd, Ringwood, Victoria, Australia
Penguin Books Canada Ltd, 10 Alcorn Avenue, Toronto, Ontario, Canada M4V 3B2
Penguin Books (NZ) Ltd, 182–190 Wairau Road, Auckland 10, New Zealand

Penguin Books Ltd, Registered Offices: Harmondsworth, Middlesex, England

First published 1980
11 13 15 17 19 20 18 16 14 12

Text copyright © Allan Ahlberg, 1980
Illustrations copyright © Faith Jaques, 1980

Educational Advisory Editor: Brian Thompson

Printed and bound in Great Britain by
William Clowes Limited, Beccles and London
Set in Century Schoolbook by Filmtype Services Limited, Scarborough

ISBN Paperback 0 14 03.1245 5
ISBN Hardback 0–670–80583–1

Tess   Tilly   Trixie

Mr Tick the teacher
lived in a big house
with his wife and children.
His wife's name was Mrs Tick.
The children's names were:
Tim, Tom and Teddy;
Tilly, Trixie and Tess.

Tom   Tim   Teddy

Mr Tick worked in a little school.
It was so little, it had only
one teacher – that was Mr Tick.
And it had only six children.
Can you guess who they were?

Every morning at half-past eight,
Mr Tick kissed Mrs Tick
and went off to school.
Every morning at ten to nine,
the children waved goodbye to Mrs Tick
and went off to school too.
At nine o'clock
the children lined up in the playground
and went into the classroom.

Then Mr Tick called the register.

"Tim!"

"Here, Daddy."

"Tom!"

"Here, Daddy."

"Teddy!"

"Here, Daddy."

"Tilly!"

"Not here, Daddy," said Tom.

"She forgot her dinner-money.

She went back to get it."

"Trixie!"

"Here, Daddy."

"Tess!"

"Here, Daddy."

After that the children
had their lessons with Mr Tick.
In the morning they had
reading, writing and arithmetic.
In the afternoon they had
singing, cooking and games.

At half-past three the children said
good afternoon to Mr Tick
and went home.
Mrs Tick was waiting for them
by the garden gate.
"Hallo, Mummy!" the children said.

"Hallo, Tim!
Hallo, Tom!
Hallo, Trixie!
Hallo, Tilly!
Hallo, Tess!" said Mrs Tick.
Then she said, "Where is Teddy?"
"He was cheeky to the teacher,"
said Tilly.
"Daddy kept him in."

So the days went by at the little school.
And they were happy days.
The children liked the teacher.
The teacher liked the children.
The parents were pleased with
the school.
The school was pleased with
the parents.

Then, one morning Mrs Tick
was reading the newspaper.
"Oh dear," she said. "Listen to this:
'LITTLE SCHOOLS MUST CLOSE
    An inspector will visit
    all little schools.
    If a school does not have
    enough children, it will
    be closed down.
    The children will go to a
    bigger school.'"

"That's bad news," said Mr Tick.
"You children will lose a school,
and I will lose a job!"
"What we need is more children,"
said Mrs Tick.
"Yes," said Mr Tick. "But where from?"
All of a sudden Tilly said,
"I have an idea!"
She whispered it to Teddy.
"That's a good idea," said Teddy.
He whispered it to Mr Tick.
"That *is* a good idea," said Mr Tick.
He began to laugh.
"We will do it!"

The next day the children
had some surprising lessons
in Mr Tick's class.
They had dressing-up lessons,

and making-faces lessons,

and riding-their-bikes-in-school lessons,
and eating-lots-of-dinners lessons.

Mr Tick took some old desks
from the school shed.
Mrs Tick put up more pegs
in the school cloakroom.
Can you guess what was going on?

Two days later, the inspector arrived.
Mr Tick met him at the school gate.
"The children are working in groups
this morning," he said.
"Come and see!"
Mr Tick took the inspector
round the school.

In the classroom he said,
"Here we have the reading group."

In the playground he said,
"Here we have the games group."

In the hall he said,
"Here we have the singing group."

On the school field he said,
"Over there we have the
cross-country running group."

Can you guess
who all the children were?
Well, the inspector could not.
He said, "This is all very good!"
And he put it down in his notebook.

At playtime the inspector had
a cup of tea with the secretary.
Can you guess who she was?
After play he saw some more groups.

At dinner-time Mr Tick took
the inspector into the hall again.
"Here the children are having
their dinners," he said.
"It is self-service."

Then the inspector had
a cup of coffee with the cook.
Can you guess who she was?

And he said,
"Well, Mr Tick, there is no need
to close *this* school.
You have plenty of children!"
Then he shook hands with Mr Tick
and said goodbye.

After that Mr Tick gave the cook
and the secretary a big kiss.
He gave the reading group,
the games group, the singing group
and the cross-country running group
a big hug.

And he gave a half-day's holiday
to the six cleverest
and most hard-working children
in the whole school.
And you can guess who they were!

The End